Double Shift

Van Cole

Published by Van Cole, 2022.

DOUBLE SHIFT

First edition. December 30, 2022.

Copyright © 2022 Van Cole.

ISBN: 979-8223627944

Written by Van Cole.

Table of Contents

Double Shift
MMM First Time Hockey Romance

By: Van Cole

By: Van Cole

Foreword

Harvey Price is the best player in the league but he's playing for the wrong team.

He's known as hockey's playboy. Every time he goes into a bar, he finds someone new to flirt with. That is until he meets Jay Collins, the new defenseman for his team and his potential replacement.

His usual approach doesn't work on Jay because, well, he's smitten. But Harvey Price can't be gay. He's known for chasing skirts and yet, he cannot deny that Jay is the best-looking thing he's seen in a while.

And then there's the fitness trainer. Oh, he is too.

And Harvey is left with a three-way tie.

Will he stick to the straight and narrow?

Or will he go for the handsome young hockey player gunning for his position?

Or maybe work up a sweat with his personal trainer during after-hours?

Whatever his choice, this book is bound to melt right through the ice.

Double Shift

Chapter 1 Harvey

"Another whiskey, sir?"

"Mhm, and maybe your number, too," I said with a wink.

The bartender, a young blonde, smiled. Her cheeks were a rosy shade of red. Apparently, asking for her number was enough to make her blush. As she bit her bottom lip with embarrassment, her eyes wandered along my body. Did she like what she saw? "I'm flattered, I really am, but I can't do that while I'm at work."

"Oh, come on, it'll be our little secret. Just write it down on a napkin or something – no one has to know." I paused to lean forward. "I promise you won't regret it." My voice lowered to a soft, seductive tone that could barely be heard over the jukebox.

Again, she smiled. "Here you are, sir." She said as she handed over my drink.

"Tell me, do you know who I am?" I asked as I ran my finger along the rim of my glass.

"Of course." She answered. "Everyone in this town knows who you are." She tilted her head toward the TV. "The Minute Men are always on."

I grinned. "So, you're a fan, then."

"Not particularly but my dad's a fanatic. Sometimes, I can't get him to shut up about hockey." She rolled her eyes. "Dads, what are you going to do, right?"

"Say, what's your name?" I asked after taking a swig of whiskey. Top shelf. Nice and smooth.

"Melody."

"Melody," I repeated, nodding my head. "My, that's a lovely name."

Her cheeks reddened once more, even darker this time around. I could tell by the look in her eye – that glisten of excitement – that I was slowly getting through to her. Good. By the end of the night, she would be mine.

"And, do you know what would be really swell, Melody?"

"What's that?" She asked, raising an eyebrow in question.

"If you went on a date with me." She was about to say something but I held up my hand to hold her off. "Think about it. Your dad would go absolutely nuts if he knew you rejected the Harvey Price – star defensemen of the Minute Men."

"Well, aren't you a modest one." Her tone turned cold. With her arms crossed against her chest and her lips pressed into a thin, hard line, she looked rather disappointed.

"What can I say?" I chuckled before downing my drink. "So, is that a yes?"

"I'm sorry but the answer is no."

"What?" I furrowed my brows together in confusion. No one had downright rejected me before.

"I can't go on a date with you."

"Why not?"

Melody leaned in nice and slow. As she did so, her shirt dipped down exposing the upper part of her chest. Instinctively, my gaze lingered on her cleavage, drinking in the wonderful sight before me. She was pretty well endowed with nice, perky breasts. A D-cup, maybe. And yet... they weren't doing anything for me. Usually, I'd be hounding over a girl like this but... nothing.

It must be the whiskey.

"I don't exactly play for the right team, so to speak." Melody glanced over at her fellow bartender. She was also cute with a bubble butt hugged tightly by a pair of yoga pants.

"Lesbian?" I guessed with a dumbfounded look plastered on my face.

"Mhm. Been dating for three months now. I know it's pretty early for me to say something like this but I really do think I found the one." She sighed a contented sigh. "There's just something about her, you know? It's like every time I see her, someone zaps me with a defibrillator – heart goes all crazy." Her eyes glazed over. "And don't even get me started on the sex."

My mind wandered, picturing the two women sharing a bed together. Most straight men would find that sort of thing completely irresistible. It can get them hard in a heartbeat. And yet... I was as soft as melted butter.

What was wrong with me?

"You know, the funny thing is I thought I was straight before I met Sadie."

"Really?" I asked. "I find that hard to believe."

She nodded. "It's true. I dated jocks and the like. The sex was decent but I always felt like there was something missing. As it turned out, I was playing for the wrong team." She giggled and once again looked over at Sadie. Her whole face was alit with glee.

"I see," I said not quite sure how to respond properly. I had never understood how people could just switch their sexual orientation. You either like boys or you like girls – it's as easy as that.

And I like girls.

***

"Price!" My coach, Mr. Morrison, hollered as soon as I stepped into the locker room. "You're late, as always. You missed our huddle."

"It's fine." I dismissed his comment as I headed for my locker.

He narrowed his eyes, lips pressed together in a disapproving grimace. "Have you been drinking again? I told you to cut the shit."

"I had a couple of shots this afternoon. Relax. I'm sober."

"You better be." He growled. "If you keep testing me like this, I will cut you from the team."

"I'm sure you will." I snickered sarcastically. "This team would fall apart without me and you know it."

"Alright, tough guy." Mr. Morrison stepped forward, glaring at me with a steely expression. He was approaching fifty and he already sported a full head of gray hair. He wouldn't last much longer. "Let's see how much longer you stick around with that rotten attitude." And, with that, he walked away.

The locker room was eerily silent in his wake. All the other players were stealing glances in my direction. That's right. I'm not afraid of the coach – or anyone else for that matter.

Just then, someone emerged from the showers, steam rolling off their body.

A new guy.

A fucking sexy new guy.

To my surprise, my cock jumped to life at the sight of him. It throbbed with excitement as I took in the sight of his broad shoulders, the lean taper of his waistline, and his chiseled midsection. Damn.

He looked up and our eyes locked.

The air became thick – so thick that it was impossible to breathe.

Fuck. What was happening right now?

My body felt like it was on fire.

"Hey." He said, his voice nice and husky. The sound of it sent a shiver running down my spine. "You must be Harvey. I'm a big fan." The stranger held out his hand, letting go of his towel in order to do so. As a result, it fell to the ground, exposing his manhood.

Now, this sort of thing happens all the time inside a locker room. I've seen a guy's junk a thousand times before but this time around it sparked something deep inside of me. My cock twitched with excitement. It hardened. My heart thumped. Beads of sweat formed at the back of my neck.

What the fuck was wrong with me?

"Yeah," I answered, trying to play it cool. "The one and only."

The handsome young man rushed to grab his towel, cheeks coloring with embarrassment. "Sorry." He mumbled.

"Don't worry about it. Happens a lot around here." I slapped his shoulder. For some reason, I allowed my hand to linger on his body, enjoying its smoothness. A tingle crept through my arm, decorating my skin with goosebumps.

"Still, what a way to make a first impression, right?" He chuckled. "Anyway, I'm Jay Collins, the new defenseman." Jay stood a few inches shorter than me, forcing him to look up while we spoke. His long eyelashes fluttered as his soft caramel eyes melted right through me.

No, what the hell am I thinking?

This is my teammate. This is ridiculous. I can't possibly be attracted to another man – let alone this one.

"Quit the chit chat, girls, it's time to get on the ice!" Coach Morris called from the doorway as he clapped his hands. "Last one out is doing fifty laps."

Everyone groaned and rushed forward. I hadn't even changed yet. Quickly, I grabbed my uniform and started to put it on. Before I knew it, Jay and I were the only ones left. I growled. I wasn't about to run fifty laps for that asshole.

"Hey, you better let me get out there first," I said. "Seniority rights and all."

"That hardly seems fair." Jay protested. "I don't want to run the fifty laps. I hate running."

"Well, tough luck because today you get to be a track star." I snatched his uniform and threw it into the showers. It landed in a large puddle of water. Snickering, I exited the locker room before he could retaliate. The coach would not be happy with his tardiness. Good. One less defenseman meant less competition.

With a smug look on my face, I eased onto the ice and breathed in the frigid rink air. Ah, there's nothing like it.

Chapter 2 Jay

What an asshole.

I wrung out my clothes but they were absolutely drenched. I tried to dry them underneath the hand driers but it was pointless.

With no other choice, I threw on the wet uniform. It felt extremely gross. Already, my skin crawled with disgust.

My jaw locked with anger as I went to grab my hockey stick but it was no longer there. I opened my locker but it was empty. "Damnit." I cursed underneath my breath. "Don't tell me that bastard took it." I slammed the door shut and stomped out to the ice. Before I could get into the rink, the coach stopped me.

"Did you have enough time in there, princess?" He asked with a snarl. "Or should I install a vanity just for you."

"I'm sorry but –"

"Shut it. I don't want to hear your pathetic excuse." He pointed to my skates. "Take them off, you won't be needing them today."

"But, sir –"

"One more word and you'll be on the bench for the entire season. I don't care if the general manager eats me alive for the decision."

I wanted to lash out at this man. He was being completely unfair. But, at the same time, I didn't want to risk losing my position on the team. I had worked much too hard to get to the big leagues, I wasn't about to blow it now. With a bitter taste in my mouth, I bent down to unlace my skates.

Harvey rounded the edge of the rink and smirked my way. Oh, I'm not one for violence but at that moment, I wanted to wipe that dirty smirk off his face.

"Get a move on, princess." With the coach breathing down my neck, my only choice was to start running.

God, I hate running.

***

By the end of practice, I was drenched with sweat and I hadn't even stepped foot on the ice.

"Good hustle out there." Coach nodded his head in approval. "Keep this up and we're bound to win the cup."

Harvey skidded to a halt right in front of me as I wiped the sweat from my brow. "Having fun? By my count, you're only on lap 38. Twelve more to go. If you keep up your current pace you might finish by tomorrow morning."

My hands tightened into fists as I approached the plexiglass that separated us. "What the hell is your issue?" I growled through gritted teeth. "You're friendly one minute and a complete dick the next? Bipolar much?"

Harvey laughed. "Oh, you have a lot to learn."

I was about to lose my temper when someone grabbed me by the shoulder. I turned around to find the goalie. "Come on, you should probably change out of this uniform before you catch a cold. It's absolutely soaked." By the time I looked back at Harvey, he was already leaving the rink. I wanted to hate him, I really did, but at the same time, I couldn't help but notice how handsome he was. It's extremely difficult to stay angry at someone you find extremely attractive.

He disappeared from view and I snapped out of my daze.

"Hey, are you alright?"

"Yeah, yeah, I'm fine." I shrugged away the goalie and returned to the locker room. There, I thought about hitting the showers a second time but at this point, all I wanted to do was go home. My legs were on fire and they would definitely need a long ice-soak.

"Don't sweat it about Harvey. He always acts like a total dick to the newbies, especially when it comes to second defensemen."

"Well, it seems like someone needs an attitude check," I mumbled under my breath. "Who does he think he is?"

"If you ask him, he thinks that he's some sort of hockey god or something." The goalie shook his head. "But, really don't worry about it."

"Why are you lying to the kid, Chad?" Another man walked over wearing nothing but a pair of loose-fitting gym shorts. "We all know that Harvey is going to try and scare this guy off the team."

"What do you mean?" I asked as I tossed on a t-shirt. It smelled a little funny like it had stayed in the wash a bit too long.

"Harvey has a habit of driving away his competition. If you ask me, he's scared."

I ran my fingers through my hair and considered his words. "Scared, huh?"

"That's my guess, anyway. He's got a definite Napoleon complex. Smallest defenseman on the league so he's got to compensate somehow."

"Well, let's give him a run for his money." I grabbed my stick, a fire burning in my eyes. "Will you two help me train? I'll compensate you in any way –"

Chad waved his hand in dismissal. "William and I will do it – free of charge."

William nodded in agreement. "Definitely. As long as it means seeing that jerk being put in his place."

With that, the three men went back on the ice. The Zamboni was already there but the driver ignored them as he did a pass around the perimeter.

"Now, if you ask me, your best chance of upending Harvey is by playing offensively." William weaved his blade from side to side, carrying the puck along with it. "Harvey may be one hell of a defender but he's got little stats in the scoring department. That's where you will come in."

"I've never done that before..." I bit my bottom lip, uncertain. "How am I supposed to defend and play offensively at the same time?"

"Oh, come on, people do it all the time." William passed the puck to Chad who spun around, shaving ice off the ground.

"You just have to learn." Chad pointed out. "How hard can it really be?" He shot the puck into the goal. "You can multi-task, can't you?"

"I suppose..."

"Well, that's half the battle right there." Chad leaned on his stick and glided toward me.

"But, don't get so caught up in scoring that you lose sight of your original task: defending. There has to be a definite balance or you're bound to flop." William slapped my shoulders so hard, I fell forward barreling right into the Zamboni. "And, I think that's a wrap for today," William muttered. "Let's hope you don't have a concussion."

Chapter 3 Harvey

The following week.

A surge of adrenaline shot through my system as I walked into the arena. Their cheers grew louder as they noticed me. I held up my stick to rile them up even further. "Don't get a big head out there." Coach warned under his breath as he stood on the sidelines, arms crossed against his chest. "We don't need a repeat of last season."

"I got us all the way to the cup – don't forget that." I snapped.

"Yeah, and you're the reason we lost." Chad snickered in agreement with the coach. He had always been the man's little lap dog. It was disgusting.

Once I got on the ice, I glided along the edge so the crowd could get a good look at the man they'd be cheering for.

To my surprise, I caught Jay stepping into the rink.

I immediately charged toward him until our bodies were inches apart. "What are you doing here? Didn't the coach tell you that your position is on the bench?"

He faked a laugh, mocking me.

My grip tightened to the point where I thought I might splinter the shaft of my stick. Our eyes locked. Bitter rivalry thickened the air. Oh, this newbie was asking for it now.

"Mind you don't choke." He shot just before the game could start. His comment left me derailed. I was accustomed to the veteran players giving me a hard time – they were jealous, after all – but never a new guy. Usually, they were down on their knees, ready to worship me.

The thought of Jay on his knees festered in my mind. For a split second, I imagined those full lips wrapping around my cock, head bobbing up and down. But it wouldn't stop there. He would add his tongue to the mix, letting it run along the underside of my member.

I was so lost in my own fantasies that I barely registered the puck flying my way. Luckily my ear was so attuned to the whizz of plastic flying over the ice that I immediately perked up and managed a solid defense. The other team groaned with defeat as I passed the puck, allowing us to score.

My euphoria didn't last long. I couldn't even hear the crowd cheer. I was much too preoccupied with the fact that I had just fantasized about Jay giving me a blow job – and worse yet, I had liked it. My dick throbbed against the cup I wore and I had to admit, it was rather painful.

"And, would you look at that! A shot made by first defenseman, Jay Collins!" The sportscaster broke through my worries. "That's his second shot this game – very impressive!"

I shot a glare at the young man but he didn't seem to notice or he was downright ignoring me. My teeth mashed together with frustration as I saw him making shot after shot. People started to chant his name. The sound grew louder and louder, penetrating through my skull.

"Collins, a recruit from Boston, seems to have been the perfect pick for this team. This is their best game in a long, long time. Paired with Price's killer defense, the opposing team doesn't stand a chance." The sportscaster had no qualms with singing this man's unwarranted praises. It was his first major-league game. This was nothing more than beginner's luck.

Jay did a little victory lap as he scored his tenth point for the game. Big whoop. His cockiness was really starting to piss me off. I was supposed to be the show-off of the team, not this twerp.

Out of the corner of my eye, I saw someone running up the ice, puck between his blade. Jay was too busy gloating to even notice. The brute got right past him and up to the goalie line where he had no trouble making the shot.

"And a horrible upset for Collins!" I didn't bother to listen to the rest of the sports caster's outburst. I already had Collins pinned to the side of the rink, stick against his neck.

"What the fuck is wrong with you?" I snarled, feeling like a rabid animal about to snap. "How about you stop playing the hero and get your head out of your ass."

He laughed. "That's saying a lot coming from the likes of you." He shoved me off. I was surprised by the amount of power he had hiding in those taut muscles of his.

Rage consumed me as I threw the first punch. It caught him right in the jaw. He stumbled back and wobbled on his legs, seconds away from collapse. Before he could regain his composure, I tackled him into the wall.

What pissed me off even more was that he wouldn't fight back. His hands were balled into fists but he wouldn't use them. "Too much of a wimp to hit me?" I spat as I threw yet another punch.

He was fast – faster than I expected. He ducked just in time for me to bash my hand against the thick plexiglass.

I spun around but instead of finding Jay I found a referee blowing his whistle. I was dragged off the ice and thrown into the penalty box for five minutes. A loud boo echoed through the arena as soon as the door was shut.

Fuming, I was forced to watch the game from the box. Coach Morrison sauntered up to me with this smug look on his face. "Did someone lose his cool?"

I ignored the old man and narrowed my gaze at the defenseman gunning to replace me. As much as I hated to admit it, he was actually pretty good. Despite being a rookie, he could hold his own on the ice. Even when opposing players attempted to barrel into him, he always managed to keep his balance.

As the minutes ticked away, I found myself mesmerized. He moved with such grace that it was hard to look away. A lustful heat filtered through my body and settled into my chest. My eyes wandered every inch of his body wondering what he would like with that uniform of his on my bedroom floor – his body naked and vulnerable on my bed.

The thought excited me.

I delved deeper into my fantasies and imagined my hands gliding along his silken skin. Or, his lips on mine. Better yet, our bodies locked together, hip to hip –

The ref snapped in my direction and waved me back onto the ice. My cheeks were red with embarrassment. I was straight so what was I doing imagining this guy in bed with me and why the hell did I like it?

The question bothered me so I did what I could to avoid him but my eyes kept wandering that way. I just couldn't look away.

***

The game ended with us smashing the opposing team. Frankly, they didn't stand a chance.

I was about to head into the locker room when I noticed Jay lingering by the stands. He was signing some kid's skate. The kid had the brightest smile on his face as Jay tousled his hair.

"Seems like you already have a fan," I commented as I leaned against the locker room entrance. "I bet you just made that kid's day."

Jay shook his head. "I don't need the flattery. I can tell you don't like me and that's fine by me."

I stepped forward until we were standing a few inches apart. "Look, I know we probably hit it off on the wrong foot but I want to be the better man here and offer my apologies." I held out my hand. "And I suggest you accept that apology because it isn't every day that Harvey Price does something like this."

"Does Harvey Price know he sounds like a condescending asshole right now?" Jay crossed his arms against his chest. "That kind of attitude isn't going to work with me."

I sighed. "What do you want me to do? Get down on one knee?"

"Now that's a thought." He said with a naughty little smirk that lit up his entire face. "I might even like that?"

"What?" I sputtered. Was he implying something?

"Oh, nothing." He started forward but I grabbed his wrist and reeled him back.

"Look, before you go, I just wanted to let you know that you actually did a good job out there and that the team is lucky to have you."

I couldn't tell for sure but it looked like he was blushing and blushing hard. Even the tips of his ears looked a little red. "Thanks." He mumbled under his breath. "You weren't half bad yourself. And man, you really know how to throw a punch."

"Sorry about that. I'm known for having a bad temper when I'm on the ice. Hopefully, we can move past that." I held out my hand. "What do you say?"

He hesitated but nonetheless, he shook my hand.

I squeezed his hand against mine as I felt a current of electricity buzzing through my limbs. There was just something about this man...

"Hey, how about we grab a couple of drinks? I know this local place – it has the best tap in town."

"Aren't we supposed to stay off the alcohol during the season?" He raised his eyebrow in question. "If the coach finds out..."

"He won't. Don't sweat it." I said with a wink. "And quit being such a newbie. Rules are meant to be broken, you know."

Chapter 4 Jay

At the bar.

"Would you look at those two." Harvey pointed across the bar at a couple of redheads who had just walked in. "You think they're sisters or friends?"

I squinted in their direction but it was too dark to tell. "I don't know. Why does it matter anyway?"

"Why does it matter?" Harvey shook his head like I had just asked the stupidest question in the universe. "I can't believe you just asked me that."

"What?"

"If they are sisters then they are less likely to agree to a threesome –"

"Threesome?" I nearly choked on the word. "Who said anything about a threesome? I thought we were here to enjoy a couple of drinks."

Someone snorted nearby. "I'm sorry." The bartender hid her mouth behind her hand. "It's just that what you said just now was really funny."

I furrowed my brows together in utter confusion. "I'm sorry but I have no idea what's going on right now..."

She grabbed my glass and replaced it with a new one. Harvey nodded as she placed it on his tab. "You see, Harvey is a womanizer. He tries to get inside the pants of every girl he sees."

"Not every girl." He corrected. "Only the cute ones."

"Well, let's just say that his standards aren't very hard because he'll pretty much go for anyone with a couple of legs to spread." She continued. "He tried flirting with me a couple of weeks ago but then I finally told him I was already taken."

"As much as I beg, Melody and her girlfriend won't join me in bed." He groaned like it was the end of the world. "I swear, women can be so cruel."

"You're really into the threesome thing, huh?" I asked. For some reason, the liquor tasted bitter in my mouth. All I could think about was this handsome man sharing his bed with all of these women. It felt wrong. It should have been me in that bed. I bit my bottom lip to hold back the crushing sense of disappointment. Who was I kidding? Of course he was straight. I was a fool for ever thinking he could be gay.

"It's every man's dream, isn't it? To have two gorgeous girls at the same time." He chuckled. A second later, he was up on his feet. With a swagger to his step, he approached the two girls. By the way they giggled, I could tell he was sweet talking them with ease.

"He'll be back." The bartender said a minute after he left. "He's always like this. He flirts with everyone but I never actually see him taking anyone home."

I looked over at her nametag. It read 'Melody.'

"How long have you known him for?" I asked.

"Not for very long but it doesn't take long to understand a man like that." She wiped down the counter beside me. Her shirt was especially low-cut, exposing the upper half of her breasts. "And it's not that difficult to read you, either." She said with a knowing smile. "You like him, don't you?"

I nearly dropped my glass. "Where did you get that idea from?"

"The way you look at him. I can tell that you're interested but at the same time, you're holding yourself back. If you ask me, I think you should tell him how you feel." She poured out a glass of wine and handed it over to a blonde. "He's over there."

"I know." She answered. "I'm waiting for the redheads to leave."

"That's not usually your style." Melody commented with a grin. "You usually just charge right in there."

"Doesn't hurt to change the tactics from time to time." She sipped her wine as she looked over at Harvey with a hawk-like attention.

"What was all that about?" I asked in a whisper.

"That's Jamie. She's nuts over Harvey but he doesn't feel the same way. If he ever wanted to get laid, she's his one-way ticket and yet, he's always telling her no." Melody explained.

"Maybe he just doesn't like her," I suggested.

"Maybe, but if you ask me, all this flirting he does, it's just a way of compensating for something else."

"What do you mean?" I cocked my head in question.

"What I mean is that he's insecure about something – about who he likes and who he doesn't like."

Before I could ask her to explain, she walked away to tend to someone else. Her words jumbled around in my head. What was she talking about?

Just then, Harvey returned to the bar. "No luck." He said with a heavy sigh. "Better luck next time."

As I thought of something to say, Jamie appeared out of thin air and plopped right into Harvey's lap. She wrapped her arms around his neck and giggled. "Did you miss me?"

The sight of her made my skin crawl. I wanted to shove her off and tell her that Harvey was mine. Jealousy burned inside of me, making it hard to breathe. I was holding my glass so hard that I thought it would shatter.

"Jamie." His voice was ice cold as he held her by the hips. "I've told you once and I'll tell you again – leave me alone."

She pouted her protest. "Why are you always so mean to me, Harvey? I always see you flirting with the other girls and here I am, throwing myself on you, and you just act like I'm a piece of chopped liver."

"I'm just –"

"Look, can't you see that he's not interested?" I rose to my feet, voice trembling. "Now, why don't you leave him alone and let him enjoy his drink?"

She narrowed her eyes with bitter hatred. "Who do you think you are?" She said in a shrill, high-pitched voice. "This is between me and Harvey so stay out of it.

"He's my teammate. So, I'm not just going to sit around while you harass him."

"Harass him?" She repeated, like I had just slapped her in the face. "I wasn't harassing anyone."

"Oh yeah?" I stepped forward. "He told you he wasn't interested and yet you linger around like an annoying little gnat." I didn't know where my words were coming from. I had never spoken to a woman in such a manner. It was like I was trying to protect Harvey even though he was more than capable of protecting himself.

"Jamie, maybe you should go." Harvey pressed his hand against the small of her back. "Let's not cause a scene." He tilted his head toward security. "You remember what happened last time, don't you?"

With a huff, she stormed out.

"Should I put her drink on your tab?" Melody asked.

"Yeah, go ahead." Harvey waved his hand in approval. "Wouldn't be the first time."

"Why do you put up with that crap?" I demanded. "If you don't like her then just tell her."

"It's not that easy." He said. "She's rather persistent. Besides, if the other girls see that she's all over me, maybe it'll make them jealous."

There was so much I wanted to say. This man was gorgeous but clearly, he would never give me a chance. He was much too busy chasing skirts. Still, my heart did not want to give up on the idea. Maybe, just maybe, I could convince him to join the other team – that gay men could have just as much fun as straight men. And oh, the fun we'd have in my bedroom. That thought was soured by the image of Jamie lying there in my stead.

With a shake of my head, I put down my drink, slamming it down a little harder than I expected

"Jay –"

"Look, it's getting late. I should probably be getting home." Before I could make it more than a few feet, someone grabbed my wrist.

Harvey.

My heart stopped as he pulled me toward his body, and our faces came crashing together, until only a few inches separated our lips. My heart buzzed with excitement as the whole world seemed to still.

"Don't go." He whispered. His dark eyes seemed to speak to mine, begging me to stay. Logically, I knew this was a bad idea but how was I supposed to deny a man who looked like a Greek God?

***

Somehow, we ended up in the VIP lounge. Harvey's drink count was getting pretty high and with each drink, his lips became looser and looser.

I paced myself with water and listened as he prattled on and on about his hockey career. I was starting to zone out with sleepiness when he leaned in and placed his hands on my thighs. "I've got to tell you something, Jay." His words were slurred. "I think you're sexy as fuck." Before I could respond, he cupped my cheek in his hand and pressed his lips against mine.

My world exploded with pleasure as our lips danced in perfect harmony.

His tongue slipped into my mouth, tangling with mine. As the kiss intensified, he pulled me onto his lap.

I moaned ever so gently as goosebumps crept along my skin. Between my legs, my cock came to life, pressing against the fabric of my jeans and begging for freedom.

Suddenly, Harvey tried to unbutton my pants. That's when I came crashing back into reality. I broke from the kiss and shook my head. "We can't – not while your drunk."

He frowned. "Why do you gotta be this way?"

"Because, if we're going to do this then I want it to be a sober thought as well." I pulled out my phone and called him a cab.

"Jay." He took my hand and laced our fingers together. "At least tell me this. Did you like it?"

I smiled. "I liked it more than you could imagine."

Chapter 5 Kalvin

A few days later.

The gym was eerily quiet as I laid out the weights and equipment for my next session. Harvey Price and some new kid on the team. From the rumors, he had done alright for himself during his first game. Now the question left to ask was whether he'd remain good enough to stay on for the entire season.

With these thoughts in mind, I lost track of the time. I forgot all about unlocking the entrance door so when I received a call from Harvey, I rushed over and allowed them into the building. "Trying to freeze us to death, are you, Kalvin?" Harvey chuckled. "I think Jay's lips were starting to turn blue."

"My apologies. I didn't realize what time it was."

"When do you ever?" Harvey shrugged off his coat, revealing a tight-fighting workout outfit that complemented his figure to utter perfection. I was practically licking my lips at the sight of him. Then came the rookie. He was a bit leaner than most but still incredibly impressive in the looks department. He had these gorgeous baby blue eyes that were to die for. "Don't mind Kalvin, he has a bit of a staring problem."

I blushed. "Well, no use in wasting any more time. Let's get to work." I clapped my hands together. "Harvey, you should already be familiar with your new routine –"

"On it." He called as he headed over to the free weights.

"Now, you." I turned toward the rookie and I must admit, the more I looked at him, the more handsome he became. Those eyes – they were definitely my kryptonite. "Have you ever worked out with a personal trainer before?"

"No." He answered. "But I'm no stranger to the gym."

"What do you do on a typical day?"

"I start off on the treadmill –"

"Ah, that explains the lithe figure." I snatched the tape measure from around my neck and approached him, almost with an air of caution. "May I?"

"Do what you got to do." He said.

I circled around him and got a good view of his backside for the first time and, oh baby, was it fine. I bit my bottom lip, eyes drinking in the wonderful sight. It was nice and round – perfect if you asked me. I had the sudden urge to reach out and slap it but I didn't want to get charged with sexual harassment my first day with the guy.

"We'll need to bulk you up a bit if you want any chance of surviving with the big boys," I said as I wrapped the tape measure around certain parts of his body. "But, don't worry, a few months with me and I'll have you looking like a new man." I flashed a smile in an attempt to up the charm.

He returned the smile with one of his own and it was enough to pierce right through my soul. My heart skipped a beat at the sight of it.

***

By the end of the day, I had him at the deadlifts. I spotted him as he pushed his limits, sweat dripping down the side of his face. "Careful, don't strain yourself now."

Harvey chuckled. "You still have a long way to go, kid."

He heaved and managed one more rep but I could tell he was completely spent. I tossed him a rag so he could clean himself off. "What a way to work up a sweat, huh?"

"I can think of better ways..." His voice was smooth and seductive. I swear there was a hidden meaning behind his words like he was trying to tell me something. His eyes shown with mischief. It almost seemed like he had something naughty on his brain.

I blushed crimson. Could that something naughty have anything to do with me? As I considered it, I glanced over at Harvey who was downing a bottle of water. From the start, I had sported a crush for the sexy second defenseman but it was clear he wasn't interested in the same sex. Harvey was as straight as straight could be. Me, on the other hand? I was as straight as a circle.

"Thanks... by the way." Jay winked in my direction as he took off his shirt. It took every ounce of my willpower to keep from whistling. I shifted my stance to hide the bone already forming inside my boxers.

"Of course." I stuttered as my tongue failed me. "Don't mention it." That glint in his eye made me wonder. Did Jay play for my team or Harvey's? Could it be possible that he was actually flirting with me or was I only imagining it?

"Well, are you going to stand there like an idiot or are you going to join us in the showers?" Harvey grinned like a madman. "I mean, we weren't the only ones to build up a sweat."

My heart began to race. Taking a shower alongside my clients was nothing new but the thought of being so close to these two men while they were both naked sent a shiver running down my spine. I started to imagine their bodies, slick and wet, pressed against mine. A threesome is every man's dream and I'm no different. I wanted them. Both of them.

But I had a feeling that it was only a dream. As much as I wanted it, they would never go for a guy like me.

Nonetheless, I followed them to the showers and stripped off my clothing. I managed a quick peek at Jay's cut butt before he disappeared into a stall. Harvey, on the other hand, stood right in front of me in all his glory. "You really need to work on that staring problem, Kalvin. It's going to get you in trouble one of these days." He said with a wink before walking away. I couldn't help but watch as his junk swung from side to side.

Chapter 6 Jay

I zipped up my windbreaker just as the other two stepped out of the shower. To my dismay, they both had towels wrapped around their waists. Still, I had more than enough fun imagining what was underneath.

"Now you're staring too, huh?" Harvey teased.

It was strange. He hadn't said a word about our time at the bar but, at the same time, he wasn't as cold as I expected him to be. In fact, he even seemed a little flirtatious. Although, maybe it was all in my head.

"Hey, if you guys want, we can all head back to my house to cool off. I have a pretty big pool and I never really find the time to use it." I gripped my locker door, nervous they would reject my offer.

Harvey raised an eyebrow in question. "Are you asking us on a date?"

"What? No. No!" I shook my head. "Nothing like that. I just thought…"

Kalvin jabbed him in the side. "Quit giving him such a hard time." He smiled. "We would love to."

"Good!" I nearly jumped for joy. "And, if you guys are hungry, I can fire up the grill. I'm a pretty good cook if I do say so myself."

"We already said yes, there's no need to convince us any further," Harvey said with a laugh as he dropped his towel to the ground and started to get dressed.

I noticed that Kalvin's jaw nearly hit the ground. He glanced in my direction and our gazes crossed. I could tell we were both thinking the same thing. Could it be that our personal trainer was also gay and that he had the hots for Harvey, just like me?

***

"This is a pretty nice place you've got here," Kalvin commented with a smile as he sat down on the edge of the water. "The water is nice and warm, too."

"I keep it heated to a toasty 82 degrees," I said while firing up the grill.

"That must cost you a fortune." He leaned back and looked up at the stars. "I need to tell you something..." He trailed off and looked over his shoulder like he was waiting for Harvey to come flying out of the bushes. "Before Harvey comes back, that is."

"What's that?" I asked as I scraped the grill. The smell of burnt charcoal wafted up to my nostrils, making it hard to breathe. Once I was done, I closed the lid and joined Kalvin by the poolside.

"Well, I just want you to know that I'm... well, I'm gay." He looked away as if embarrassed by his sexual orientation.

I took his hand and squeezed it against mine. "I know. I saw the way you looked at Harvey – that hunger in your eye."

Kalvin frowned. "Yeah, but I'm only wasting my time. Everyone knows that he's straight. I don't have a chance in hell with a guy like that."

"I wouldn't be so sure," I said with a smirk plastered on my face. "A few nights ago, he kissed me."

It almost looked like Kalvin's eyes would bug right out of their sockets. "Are you being serious? Harvey actually kissed you?"

"Mhm." My smirk deepened with smugness. "Although, he was a little drunk so I'm sure that had something to do with it. He hasn't really mentioned it since but I'll take the fact that he doesn't hate me as a good sign, right?"

"Definitely." He stared at the water. "I have to admit, I'm a little jealous. You wouldn't believe how long it's been since I've kissed someone. I'm actually embarrassed."

"Don't be." I don't know what came over me but suddenly I had Kalvin's face in my hands and I was reeling him in for a kiss. Our lips collided with a fiery passion that left me absolutely breathless.

He returned the kiss with a hungry fervor. Already, his hands began to roam along every inch of my body.

"Mmm." Instead of pulling away, he kissed me even harder. My head started to spin but I didn't dare pull away. It felt much too good.

The screen door creaked open and we quickly severed the kiss. Harvey emerged from the house holding a pack of beers in his hand. "You were hiding these from me! I had to go searching in your basement." He shook his head, popped one open, and downed half of it. "Well, let's get this party started." A wild grin painted his face as he ran over to the diving board.

Kalvin and I could only watch as his toned muscles became taut with anticipation. And then, he was flying through the air, his body arched in the perfect angle before slicing through the water. He surfaced a few seconds later with this joyful look on his face. "I haven't done that in a while!" He shouted loud enough for the neighbors to hear. If he kept that up, I would have a civil complaint on my hands. But, honestly, I didn't care. Simply having Harvey in my pool, getting nice and wet, was enough for me.

With this thought, I got up and threw some patties on the grill. The fat sizzled against the flames as I seasoned them with the perfect amount of spices. "How do you like your meat?" I asked without really thinking about it.

Harvey laughed. "Careful, Jay, you might give Kalvin the wrong idea."

But our eyes had already locked and I knew exactly what we would be doing that evening.

***

We waited until Harvey dozed off by the fire. Only then did we make our getaway. I pushed him onto the bed and pounced. With his wrists pinned above his head, I swooped in for a kiss. His lips were seriously addictive and the more I tasted him, the more I wanted him.

He pushed his hips into the air so they could grind against mine. Already, things were getting hot and heavy and the night was only starting. I moved my lips to the side of his neck and sucked on that sensitive skin until I heard him moan with pleasure.

I released his wrists only to slip one of my hands down his pants. There, I found his hardening member. I squeezed it, forcing another moan through his lips. He arched his back with pleasure as I stroked it nice and slow. To tease him even further, I reached my other hand up his shirt and took his nipple between my fingers. I rolled it back and forth until it was painfully hard.

And then, I stopped.

He whimpered, looking up at me with a pair of puppy dog eyes. "Jay..." He whispered as he wrapped his arms around my neck, trying to pull me closer.

I smirked as I imagined everything I would do to this man – the sounds of his screams – that euphoric look on his face. With these thoughts in mind, I tore off his clothing. They went flying across the room, landing here and there.

Quickly, he returned the favor. My cock sprung to attention the second it was freed from the confines of my pants. I leaned down and took one of his nipples into my mouth.

And then that's when Harvey walked in. "What the fuck?" He shook with anger, eyes narrowing in our direction. His hands were balled up into a couple of fists. I wouldn't be surprised if he punched a hole through the wall. "I don't even know what to say right now..." His voice wavered.

"Harvey..." I called out but he was already gone. I could hear the pounding of his footsteps against the hardwood floor followed by the slamming of the front door.

Great, now the night was ruined.

Chapter 7 Harvey

A few days later, at their following game.

I was playing like absolute shit. I couldn't concentrate and it was even harder with Jay only a few feet away from me. I kept looking his way and seeing him in bed with Kalvin. The problem was that the scene didn't disgust me as it should have. Instead, it excited me.

The puck came flying my way and I moved to defend its advance but I was too slow. An opposing member charged in my direction and took me off balance. I slammed into the ground like a turtle falling on its shell.

"What a horrible upset! We haven't seen Price play this badly since his rookie days. What is going on out there?"

Coach Morrison blew his whistle, calling a timeout.

As soon as I was back on my feet, he beckoned me toward the sidelines. "Sit down." He barked. "You're eating shit today, what's wrong with you?"

I didn't bother to answer him. On any other day, I would have argued the call but I knew he was in the right. So, I simply hung my head and sat there, utterly miserable. As soon as I closed my eyes, I thought about them.

They were unbelievably sexy. In those few short seconds, I had been able to memorize every curve of their bodies. They were perfect. Even now, my cock strained to get to a level of hardness.

I wasn't angry at them for sleeping together – I was angry at myself. I was supposed to be straight and yet, I had the hots for a couple of dudes. It didn't make any sense. And yet, it was exactly what I wanted. I wanted to feel their bodies pressed against mine. My cock inside one of their tight holes. Oh, I wanted it – and I wanted it bad.

A threesome is every man's dream but I never thought I'd want one with two other men.

My chest tightened with turmoil. I didn't know what to think. If I gave in to these urges and experimented with my sexuality, what would it mean for my hockey career? It was a masculine sport. No one would support a gay hockey player. But would I be able to keep it a secret or would someone find out and expose me for who I really was.

I bit my bottom lip.

Was that a risk I was willing to take?

***

The end of the game came sooner than I expected it to. I guess I must have zoned out.

I glanced at the score.

We had lost and it was all my fault. If only I had been able to keep it together... A bitter taste formed in my mouth, overwhelming my taste buds. I felt like I would vomit at any minute. I held a hand across my stomach as it churned like some sort of circus acrobat.

The team was getting off the ice as I slipped into the locker room. I quickly threw on a fresh set of clothes and high-tailed it out of there. I didn't want to face their disappointment.

Outside, I breathed in the fresh air as I leaned against my car. The frigidness of the night air helped to clear my mind. It was obvious – I was gay – and as much as I wanted to run from it, I couldn't.

"Harvey!" I looked up to find Jay jogging in my direction.

I thought about getting in my car and driving away but for some reason, my body would not move. I was stuck in place, eyes locked with his. My heart skipped a beat as he took me by the chin and kissed me.

The kiss intensified with each passing second. I didn't even care that we were out in the open. All that mattered were those sweet, sweet lips of his.

He pushed me against the car and I could feel his bulge pressing against mine.

I was about to pull away when he bit my bottom lip and pulled at it. It sent a shiver down my spine that left me absolutely breathless. How could one man be so sexy? It didn't even seem humanly possible.

Finally, just when I thought I would pass out from the lack of air, he pulled away and looked into my eyes. "I want to be completely honest with you..." His voice was ragged. "I like you both and I want you both."

A bit of jealousy flared within me. Frankly, I didn't want to share. I wanted this man all to myself. But, at the same time, I couldn't deny the fact that being with them both was unbelievably sexy.

"You said it yourself, a threesome is every man's dream." His grin deepened. "So, if you're up to it, be at my house tomorrow at seven." With that, he winked and walked away, leaving me in a lust-filled haze.

Oh, I wanted it – I wanted it bad. But would having a threesome be diving in too deep? I didn't even know if I was truly gay or not... Or rather, if I liked gay sex.

I paced, trying to clear my head but it was in such a fog that I couldn't think straight. So, I sat in my car for a while before finally driving home. I would definitely need to sleep on it.

Chapter 8 Jay

"Do you think he's going to show up?" Kalvin asked.

"I think so," I answered. "If that kiss we had in the parking lot meant anything to him, that is…" Now I was starting to harbor my own doubts. After all, why would Harvey agree to such a thing? If word ever got out, it would ruin his career." I busied myself by grabbing a water from the fridge.

Before I could even open it, there was a knock on the door. My heart felt like a sledgehammer pounding against my chest as I walked over to open the door.

To my surprise, Harvey grabbed me and slammed me against the wall as soon as the door swung open. His lips were like fire against my own.

My mind swirled with excitement as my lungs burned.

He pushed me away and stood there with a mischievous grin on his face. "I'm done hiding from who I really am." He said. Just then, he grabbed Kalvin by the wrist and reeled him into his body. "Today's your lucky day because today's the day your crush finally admits that he's into you." He placed his hand on the small of Kalvin's back, leaned him backward and kissed him – hard.

I was getting a boner just looking at them. Unable to wait a moment longer, I rushed into the bedroom. My clothes were off by the time I made it to the nightstand. I grabbed my bottle of lube. I had a feeling we were going to need it – and lots of it.

Harvey came walking in with Kalvin cradled against his chest. He threw the man down on the bed and pounced.

I got on the bed behind him and slowly started to take off his clothes. I took my time with the task. My fingers danced across his body, savoring the feel of his muscles rippling underneath his skin. Once his shirt was lying on my bedroom floor, I leaned forward and decorated his shoulder blades with kisses.

Kalvin moaned as Harvey stroked him. The pace increased, faster and faster until his moans turned into screams.

Quickly, Harvey turned him around and tore at his clothing like some sort of wild animal. "I should have done this ages ago..." He whispered under his breath as he grabbed some lube and slathered it around his cock. It really was massive. Honestly, I didn't know how it would fit inside Kalvin's tiny puckered hole.

Harvey grabbed him by the shoulders and positioned himself. With one well-aimed thrust, he penetrated inside of him and thanks to the lube, it was a pretty smooth entrance. Kalvin gripped at the sheets, back arched with pleasure.

As Harvey started to fuck Kalvin properly, I moved in and pressed my middle finger against his asshole. He tensed for a moment but after a few gentle coos on my part, he eased up.

I forced the finger inside of him until it was knuckle deep. Once I was satisfied that it was deep enough, I started to twist it this way and that. I moved it faster with each passing second until I heard his sweet, sweet moan.

His balls slapped against Kalvin's as he started to lose control. With my other hand, I began to stroke Kalvin up and down. My thumb passed along his engorged tip to find it already wet with precum. I brought my thumb to my mouth and savored the taste. "Mmm."

With a little bit of lube, I added another finger to Harvey's ass. They moved in unison, stretching his tiny hole. It didn't take long before I added a third. I was relentless now. I fingered him hard and fast.

Suddenly, I pulled out, leaving him wanting more. I took the time to lather my cock and before he could realize what was happening, I took hold of his hair and used it as a leverage point as I rammed into his virgin hole.

Kalvin screamed, shooting his load.

Slowly, Harvey pulled out, breathing hard but that wasn't enough to get me to stop. I kept ramming into him over and over again.

Kalvin managed to slip away only to get on his knees before the second defenseman. He leaned his head down until his lips were wrapped around Harvey's thick shaft. I could tell that he was moving his tongue nice and slow, teasing the hockey player. So, I did the same.

I slowed to an agonizing pace. My cock twitched against his insides. I was minutes away from climax but I held back the feeling, wanting this moment to last. I kissed his neck, finding his sweet spot.

"Mmm, that feels so good." Harvey moaned.

"Once you go gay, you'll never go back," I whispered into his ear as he shivered with delight. Gently, I nibbled his earlobe.

Kalvin started to bob his head up and down while fondling Harvey's balls. Our eyes locked and I grinned down at the personal trainer. I gave in to all my desires as I lost control and I pounded into Harvey so hard that the bed started to rock.

It was too much for him to handle. He exploded into Kalvin's mouth. To my surprise, Kalvin swallowed every last drop and even licked his lips afterward. The sight was enough to take me over the edge.

I screamed with pleasure and coated Harvey's insides with my cum. Spent, I collapsed onto the bed. My lovers followed suit and we all laid there, looking up at the ceiling, unable to believe what had just happened to us.

"That was better than I expected..." Harvey said, breaking the silence. "Wow..."

I grinned. "I won't say I told you so."

Kalvin just smiled. "That was better than I had dreamed it would be."

"So, you've dreamt about me, have you?" Harvey asked, raising himself on an elbow.

"All the time."

They fell into a passionate kiss. I smiled, leaned back into a pillow, and fell asleep.

Chapter 9 Harvey

I woke up to the feeling of bright sunlight shining against my face. I groaned and attempted to hide my face against my pillow. Doing so, I became acutely aware of the two bodies lying beside me.

The room smelled of a deep musk. It eased my nerves but I was still on edge. Last night's events came crashing into me like a freight train. Did I really have a gay threesome? Worse yet, did I really enjoy it?

Slowly, I managed to get out of bed without waking the others. I stowed away in the bathroom and splashed my face with cold water. It didn't really help the situation. I was still freaking out. With all this pent-up energy surging inside of me, I paced the bathroom like some sort of caged animal.

I couldn't deny that I had loved the threesome. No other sexual experience had ever felt so good and trust me, I get around. But, at the same time, I couldn't shake the fact that something about it felt wrong. I couldn't do this. I wouldn't do this.

***

Later that day.

I was forced to turn off my phone. I just couldn't stand the number of texts and missed calls. Jay and Kalvin probably wanted answers but I wasn't ready to face them – not yet, anyway.

So, as dusk approached, I popped some headphones into my ears and headed out the door. It felt good to run. The repetitiveness of it helped to clear my mind. I was able to forget about what had happened and focus instead on pushing the pace. My arms pumped, adding to my momentum as music blared through my eardrums.

I was so lost in the motions that I didn't really pay attention to my surroundings. I rounded a corner and ended up bumping right into someone. Her body went flying forward but somehow, I managed to grab her wrist just in time. Doing so caused me to get caught up in her inertia and we both went tumbling onto the ground.

"Oomph!" She groaned as I landed right on top of her.

I blinked, about to apologize when I realized who it was. "Jamie?"

"You know, I'm gunning for you to fall for me but this is a little too literal for my taste." She said as she pressed on my chest. "Would you mind getting off me? Some people are staring."

I jumped to my feet and offered her a hand. "I'm sorry, I wasn't paying attention."

"I can see that." She brushed the dirt from her clothing. It was then that I realized how tight they were. Her leggings hugged her ass to utter perfection. Her toned stomach was exposed since she wore nothing but a sports bra to cover her torso. On top of that was a loose fitting hoodie.

Any man would be drooling over a girl like her.

And yet, there was absolutely no reaction on my part. My little, not so little, friend didn't even stir.

Could I really be gay?

My jaw tightened at the thought. Even after everything that had happened, I just couldn't believe it.

"Hey, what are you doing tonight?" I asked, my voice low and seductive.

She raised an eyebrow with suspicion. "Why do you ask?"

"Well, you want to go on a date with me, don't you? Today's your lucky day." I flashed a smile.

Instantly, her cheeks reddened to a rosy hue. "You mean it? You aren't just playing some cruel trick on me?"

"I mean it."

Her face lit up with a smile. Suddenly, she charged forward and ran right into my arms.

Somehow, I caught her just in time, hands resting on her ass as she pushed me against the wall of a nearby building. "Whoa, calm down."

She giggled. "I'm just so happy." It took her a minute but she finally settled down.

I pulled her away but kept my hands on her hips. I had to admit, it was a bit awkward to hold her. In a way, it felt unnatural.

"What do you say we head to Jinx's bar? We could grab something to eat and enjoy a few drinks together." I suggested. "Tonight. I'll pick you up at seven."

"Will you be coming in that fancy sports car of yours? What is it again? A Maserati? Is that the one with a trident as the logo?"

"Mhm." I narrowed my eyes in her direction. "Why do you ask?"

"Well... it's just that I've never been in a fancy car like that before. I don't know what it's like. And if I'm going on a date with a famous hockey player, I want the full experience, you know."

Jamie was sickeningly transparent. I could tell that all she wanted was a sugar daddy. She didn't like me at all – all she liked was my money.

"And do you mind if we go to that new Italian place in town? I know it's on the pricier side but I think you can afford it, can't you?" She giggled and twirled a piece of hair between her fingers. "Oh, you don't know how long I've been waiting for this!" She squealed.

Again, she jumped into my arms.

We bumped heads and a splitting pain radiated through my temples. I had a feeling it was about to be a long, long night.

Chapter 10 Jay

That same night.

The night air was cool but I didn't mind it. In fact, it felt pretty good against my skin. Leaning back in my lawn chair, I looked up at the stars with a sigh. It was such a beautiful sight but I had no one to share it with.

I tightened my grip around my beer as I recalled my sexual experience with both Harvey and Kalvin. It had been amazing – absolutely breathtaking – and yet, when morning came, Harvey was nowhere to be found. I had tried to call his cell countless times, to no avail. He wouldn't answer my texts either. Clearly, the threesome had been disappointing for him. But that look on his face. I could have sworn he enjoyed it.

A crow cawed nearby before swooping onto the patio. He hopped from foot to foot and cocked his head to the side, staring at me with a pair of beady eyes.

I tossed my bag of chips in his direction before heading inside. Through the screen door, I watched him enjoy the salty snack. At least one of us was happy.

My feet dragged along the hardwood floor as I made my way into the living room. With a sigh, I plopped onto the couch and turned on the TV. I flicked through the channels but there really wasn't anything to watch.

So, I pulled out my phone and texted Kalvin. "Are you doing anything tonight?"

His response came in a few minutes later. "I'm at work, why?"

"Never mind, then. I was just wondering if you wanted to hang out."

"I'm sorry, tonight's not a good night."

"It's alright, don't sweat it." I dropped my phone onto the couch cushion and closed my eyes. I couldn't stay cooped up in this house any longer or I would lose my sanity.

***

I ended up at Jinx's bar.

"You're back." Melody mused as she placed a glass of whiskey right in front of me. "Is everything alright? You're looking a little blue."

I shook my head. "I don't really want to talk about it."

Melody shrugged. "Suit yourself." She walked away, shelving some new bottles of liquor. I watched her to distract myself from the laughter that surrounded me. All these people, they seemed unbelievably happy. Most were enjoying their night with a significant other while here I was, all alone.

"Actually..." I called her over. "Do you think you could get me a plate of the chicken wings, extra spicy."

She raised an eyebrow in question. "Are you sure you want to do that? I mean, I wouldn't recommend them. I probably wouldn't give them to my dog."

"I don't care."

"Okay, spill it, what's wrong?" She demanded.

"Nothing."

She rolled her eyes. "You know, as a bartender, I'm pretty much a licensed psychiatrist. If you need to say something, speak now or forever hold your peace."

"What is this a wedding?" I muttered. "Look, it's nothing. Don't worry about it."

"Do you still want those chicken wings?" She asked.

"Yes."

She hesitated for a moment but she nonetheless slipped into the kitchen to give them my order. While I waited, I watched the hockey game playing on TV. Hockey was my passion. As a child, I used to play on the street with the rest of my friends. Then, as I got older, I joined a few teams and eventually went on to play at the college level. That's when they recruited me and so, here I am.

I always thought that making it to the big leagues would be my greatest accomplishment in life. And yet, even after reaching the top, I still felt incomplete.

"Here you are." Melody placed the plate of chicken wings beside my whiskey and scrunched her nose in disgust. "I hope you know what you're doing."

In all honesty, the wings were a dismal sight. They were saturated with some sort of hot sauce that had a peculiar yellow tinge to it. I picked one up and it slipped between my fingers and onto my lap. I cursed under my breath as it rolled onto the ground with a soft thud. I got off my bar stool to pick it up. As I did so, I noticed someone across the bar.

Harvey.

The whole world seemed to stop as my heart tightened with anguish. I clenched my teeth together as I saw the blonde from the other night hanging from around his waist. I could tell she was laughing. I could see the joy twinkling through her eyes.

My mouth grew bitter. I should have known better. Harvey would never come out of the closet. He would rather lie to himself than come out and tell the world that he liked another man. It made me sick.

I fumbled for my wallet and pulled out a couple of bills and tossed them underneath my plate. With a pair of wobbly legs, I managed to walk out to my car. I slumped against the steering wheel as tears burned at the corner of my eyes. I held them back. That man did not deserve my tears.

***

I arrived at Kalvin's gym a few minutes after closing time. Luckily, the door was still open. I walked inside and found him wiping off some of the equipment.

As soon as he heard me, he turned around and smiled. That smile deepened as he crossed the room, took me by the chin, and reeled me in for a kiss. If I was smart, I'd settle for Kalvin. Clearly, he was well-established in his sexuality and to top it off, he seemed like a pretty decent guy. Going after Harvey would just result in a bitter heartache. And yet, I couldn't even dream of letting him go. He was everything I had ever wanted.

"What's wrong?" Kalvin took my hand and squeezed it.

"I just saw Harvey with someone else..." My voice fell flat as I sat down on a nearby bench. "I know I shouldn't let it affect me this much but it just feels like he's stabbing my heart with a red-hot dagger." I shook my head, unable to understand his actions. "Tell me if I'm wrong but we all definitely enjoyed our time together."

"Well, I know I did." Kalvin nodded in agreement. "But maybe Harvey is just confused. He believed he was straight for a long time. I bet sleeping with two men came as a sort of shell-shock."

I laughed. "What is there to understand? You either like boys or you like girls."

Chapter 11 Harvey

A few days later, during their next game.

I tried to pass the puck to Jay but he missed it completely. One of our rivals swept up behind him, stole it, and drove it all the way up to the goalie. Luckily, Chad was able to make a decent save.

He shot the puck toward the center of the ice where one of our offensive players took charge and managed to score us a much-needed point.

The score was tight but we were slowly closing the gap. Just a few more points and we'd be able to take the lead. With this thought in mind, I concentrated on giving the game my absolute all. As we neared the championship, every game counted for much more and this game was no different.

Suddenly, I felt someone barrel into me. I lost my footing and ended up falling on the ground. When I opened my eyes, I was surprised to see Jay sprawled out on top of me.

Coach blew his whistle for a timeout and beckoned us both over. He had this sour grimace on his face. "What the hell is going on out there? You two are like oil and water." He snarled. "We aren't going to win this damn game if you keep this up."

"Don't sweat it," I said. "We're fine."

Jay didn't offer a word in response. I could tell by the blank expression on his face that something was bothering him and that something was me. "Jay...?" I started but I really didn't know what to say. I was still trying to sort everything out in my head. Spending time with Jamie had been a total drag. I had hated every minute of it and it certainly did not compare to the time I had spent with the guys. But I still couldn't come to terms with the fact that I was gay.

He turned his back on me and stepped on the ice. I could tell he was holding his hockey stick with incredible tightness. When I looked up at his face, his eyes were dead.

With no other choice, I went back to my position.

It was no surprise when we lost the game. There was absolutely no synergy between Jay and I. Our passes were awkward and they would often miss their mark.

"What the hell happened out there?" William asked as he shoved me to the side.

I growled and retaliated with a shove of my own.

"I'm sick of your shit. You act like you're the best player in the league but you've done nothing this season. I wouldn't be surprised if coach sacked you." He snickered. "And, if you ask me, you deserve it."

Before I could stop myself, I threw a punch.

William caught it before it could reach his face. With a pivot of his body, he had me on the ice, arm twisted at a painful angle.

"Be careful who you decide to pick a fight with – some of us know how to fight back." He said. Each of his words were laced with venom. He twisted my arm a bit more until I was forced to cry out with pain. Only then did he drop my arm and walk away.

My cheeks burned with humiliation. A few of the fans had lingered long enough to see my ass handed to me. I didn't need their prying stares. So, I rushed into the locker room as fast as I could. There, I ignored everyone else and left in silence.

Across the parking lot, I saw Jay get into his car. For a moment, I thought about letting him drive away but I just couldn't let this go unaddressed. I dashed over there and tapped on his window just as he turned on his car. I feared he would run over my toes but to my surprise, he actually rolled down the window. "What do you want?" He demanded.

"We need to talk."

"I don't have anything to talk about." He said, his tone icy.

"Look, I know I haven't been fair to you –"

Jay interrupted me with a laugh. "Fair?" He retorted. "Yeah, going out with that skank after sleeping with me and Kalvin... that was really fair." He shook his head. "I don't believe you right now..."

"Jay..."

"I get it. Maybe you're scared of what your feeling. I felt it too when I first came to terms with my sexuality but I was never such a backstabber." He put his car into reverse and eased out of the parking space. "I suggest you get your act together and decide what you want." And with that, he drove away, tires screeching against the asphalt.

I was left standing there feeling like such a jackass. What was I supposed to do? Deep down, I knew I had feelings for that man and for Kalvin too. I wanted them both but I just couldn't come to terms with it. There was just something so taboo about being gay that it scared me.

***

To blow off some steam that night, I headed over to the gym. Kalvin was eerily silent. Most of the time, he could nag my ear off but this time around, he didn't say a word. So, I was left to run on the treadmill with nothing but my music for company.

Occasionally, I would glance over at the personal trainer, looking for clues. What was going on in that head of his? Was he as pissed off as Jay was?

Just then, Jamie walked through the doors. The second she saw me, she flashed a smile.

"Go away," I said, a little more harshly than I intended.

She frowned. "What do you mean?"

"I mean..." I took a deep breath to steady my nerves. "That I'm not interested in you or any other woman." As I spoke, I hoped it was loud enough for Kalvin to hear.

"What?"

But I didn't bother to explain it to her. I simply gathered up my stuff and left.

Chapter 12 Jay

The following day, at practice.

I waited until everyone was on the ice, including Harvey. Only then did I approach the coach. "Do you think I can have a minute?"

He looked out at the team before turning his attention in my direction. "Alright." He blew his whistle. "Continue with the stretches then practice on passing. I want to see an excellent pass rate when it comes to this week's game, do you hear me?"

No one acknowledged Coach Morrison but I knew that most of them would do as he asked. Harvey would probably be the only defiant one.

"Alright, let's step into my office, shall we?" With one hand on my shoulder, he ushered me toward the bleachers. They were ice cold due to the arena's frigid temperatures. "What's on your mind, Jay?"

I took a deep breath. Honestly, I didn't know where to start. It wasn't like I could just tell him the truth. There was probably a rule against inter-teammate dating or something. "I have a problem."

"I guessed as much." He responded. "Or else you wouldn't want to talk to me."

I nodded and ran my hands along my legs, trying to soak up the sweat that had gathered along my palms. "The thing is... I think it would be better off for everyone if you traded me to another team."

"What?" He nearly choked on the word. "Why? You're panning out to be a great player."

I shook my head. "There's no need to flatter me. I understand that I have been nothing but a let down for the past few games."

He glanced over at the team and at Harvey in particular. The second defenseman was looking our way and I could tell he was trying to read our lips. I turned, hiding my face from him.

"Does this have anything to do with Harvey? I know he can be a bit of a hard-ass but I promise, you get used to him."

"Honestly, I'd rather not say." I pressed my lips together before rising to my feet.

"You should really think this over, Jay."

"Oh, trust me, I have. As much as I love it here, it isn't worth it." I spoke with a heavy heart. "When something isn't right, there's no point in forcing it."

"Then why move to another team? Is that really going to solve your problems?" The coach asked. It was clear that he wanted me to stay.

"Yes. It will."

***

I left practice early that day. Coach had promised to ask the general manager about my request.

For now, that was enough. I'd probably get the team a decent amount of money and that would undoubtedly help them in the long run. The GM would see that and trade me away from the team – away from Harvey Price.

I looked around my home. I had only lived there for a few weeks but I still loved the place. It would be a shame to leave it for something else. Still, I couldn't stand this heartache any longer.

My phone buzzed in my pants pocket. I pulled it out to see Kalvin's number on the screen. I answered it. "Hello."

"Hey." He said. "How are you holding up?"

"I'm fine." I lied. "What about you?"

"I'm okay." An awkward silence settled on the line. "How was practice? I can only imagine what it must be like..."

"Fine." Again, I had no problem lying.

"Are you okay?" Kalvin's voice was laced with worry. "Because, if you need to talk, you know I'm here, don't you?"

My throat tightened. I choked on my words. Kalvin was the kindest soul I had ever met and still, he wasn't enough for me. I wanted to give him the love he deserved but my heart belonged to another. I would be complete if I was able to live with the two of them but that would never happen.

"Jay...?"

"Sorry. I'm fine."

"Look, do you want to grab dinner or something? I know this really nice vegetarian place. They have a killer Pad Thai with this really crispy tofu recipe."

"I'm not really a tofu guy," I said. My taste buds recoiled just at the thought of it. "But thanks for the offer."

"Okay, well, maybe I can swing by your place and we can just watch a movie or something. What do you say?"

"I'm sorry, Kalvin, but I'm just not feeling it tonight. I think I'm just going to take a bath and go to bed."

"Are you sure that everything is alright?" He pressed.

"Yes, everything is alright," I answered, trying to sound as convincing as possible. I didn't give him enough time to respond before hanging up the phone.

My heart felt like it was breaking into a million pieces. I didn't want to do this. I loved being a part of the Minute Men but Harvey Price would only break my heart over and over again, that much was clear.

So, leaving was my only choice.

Chapter 13 Harvey

At the following practice.

I waited in the locker room for Jay to show up but he never did. I checked my phone to see if he had answered any of my texts but of course, he hadn't.

Where was he?

"Have any of you seen Jay?" I asked my teammates but they just shrugged in response.

"Why do you care, anyway?" Chad called out. "You're just going to run him off the team like every other defenseman. You should be happy he isn't here. He's just making your life easier."

I advanced toward the goalie, nostrils flaring. "I don't need your mockery." I snarled. "I asked a simple question. I didn't need all the back talk."

Chad rose to his full height. He was a few inches shorter than I was but his thick girth almost made him look bigger. "You know, I'm getting really sick and tired of your shit."

"Stay out of this, Chad," I said, my voice level. "All I wanted I know was where I could find Jay."

"How about you leave the kid alone?" He jabbed two beefy fingers into my chest. "How about that?"

"I can't," I said, losing my temper. "Because I love him."

The whole locker room fell into a deadly silence.

Everyone looked at me like I had just spawned a third head.

"What?" Chad shook his head with disbelief. "I must be hearing things. Did you just say that you loved him?"

"Yes." I planted my feet in the ground, arms folded across my chest. "What's so wrong with that? So what if I like another man? Sue me." Adrenaline surged through my veins like never before. It felt good to stand up for who I really was. I was done hiding.

"Ahem." Coach Morrison cleared his throat in order to get my attention.

I whipped around to find a sympathetic look on his face.

"We need to talk." He said. "Now." His seriousness took me by surprise. I had never seen him acting this way. So, I followed him out to the bleachers where we sat down together. He had some silly joke that this was his office. "I had a feeling that this had something to do with you."

"What are you talking about?" I asked, growing suspicious.

"Jay asked me to transfer him off the team."

My eyes widened. It felt like a boulder had just fallen between us, shattering everything in its wake. "Tell me you're kidding."

"I'm not." He said with a sigh. "It's a shame because he's a good player. I can tell. He needs some work but with a little bit of polish, he'll turn out alright." Coach shook his head. "But you just had to chase him away, didn't you?"

"It's not like that." I protested. "It's complicated..."

"It's always complicated with you." He sighed. "You can't take the competition."

"It's not like that!" I shouted. "This time, it's not like that at all. I love that man and I've been a fool because I've yet to tell him as much."

Coach gaped at me like some sort of dead fish. I didn't even wait for him to respond before I left the arena and jumped into my car, uniform and all. Once I was behind the wheel, I threw off my skates and drove barefoot. My mind was buzzing but one thing was for sure: I couldn't let Jay leave.

***

When I reached his home, Kalvin's car was already in the driveway. I parked right behind him and barely came to a complete stop before I was out the door. I rang the doorbell but no one answered.

"I know you're in there!" I shouted through the window. "Won't you please let me in?"

Nothing.

My heart hammered with the dread of rejection. I couldn't stand the thought of Jay hating me for the rest of his life just because I was too much of a coward to accept my own sexuality.

"Jay, I'm begging you, open up the door." I pounded on the wooden door but to no avail. "Jay..." I was just about to walk away in utter defeat when the door swung open.

I turned around and locked eyes with the one person I had ever truly loved. Without thinking, I took his face into my hands and kissed him. Our lips ignited with an inner fire that burned through my entire soul. The more I kissed him, the easier it became to accept who I was and who I was meant to be.

Our bodies came together like a couple of magnets, hips locking against one another.

My heart thumped like a drum as I gave up all my insecurities.

When my lungs started to scream for oxygen, I pulled away and looked into those beautiful eyes of his. "Jay... I need you to listen to me now."

He blinked but did not say a word.

I placed my hands on his shoulders and squeezed them. "I'm sorry. I never should have hurt you like that but I was scared. I thought I was a straight man all of my life and then you came around and turned everything upside down. I honestly didn't know what to do." I blushed with embarrassment. "After my 'date' with Jamie, I knew without a doubt that women didn't attract me. They never did – I only fooled myself into thinking I liked them. That's all it was."

Jay studied my face for a moment as if it would hold all the answers he was looking for. "And you're sure...?"

I nodded. "I can't deny it any longer. I'm gay." It felt like such a relief to say those words, like a weight had been lifted from my shoulders. I took him by the hips and pulled him a little closer. "And there's one more thing I need to say."

Nervous energy buzzed through my entire body.

"What is it?"

"I love you."

His eyes widened with surprise.

For a moment all we could do was stare at each other.

"Oh, would you two kiss already?" Kalvin called out from across the room.

And, that's exactly what we did. Somehow, his lips felt even sweeter than I remembered. I savored every second as I held him close to my chest, vowing to never let him go.

Jay pulled away and looked over at Kalvin. "This will only work if it's the three of us. I cannot love one without the other." He said. "I hope that's okay with you."

I nodded. "I won't say no to a sexy personal trainer," I said with a wink. "You know me, I like to work up a sweat."

Kalvin grinned. "So, what are we waiting for?" He tilted his head toward the bedroom. "Let's fuck and make up."

Chapter 14 Kalvin

I took them both by the hand and pulled them into the bedroom. Harvey was the one to push me onto the mattress, while Jay worked on taking off his clothes.

Harvey was just about to kiss me when he caught sight of Jay unbuttoning his shirt. He whistled, a wild smirk spreading across his face. "Oh, baby." He cat-called as he took Jay by the hips and drew him into bed with us.

As Harvey made out with the young hockey player, I got up and turned on some music. It flowed through the room, setting the mood. "What do you think you're doing?" Jay called from the bed. "Get that cute little butt of yours over here right now."

I did as he said. He shoved me back and tore at my clothes. As soon as my pants came off, he took my hardening cock into his mouth. He sucked on the tip, his tongue going around and around.

"Fuck, Jay…" I moaned with pleasure as his tongue moved around my length. He looked up at me with a pair of innocent eyes that turned my heart to mush. With his hands on my thighs, he spread my legs apart and leaned down even further until he had my balls in his mouth. "Mmm…" I cried out as he sucked them a little harder.

"Do you like that?" Harvey whispered into my ear as he squeezed my shoulders, massaging them gently. Oh, it felt good. I had never felt so pampered in my life. Why can't all relationships be like this? I thought to myself.

His lips settled on my neck as he nibbled at my sensitive flesh. He took it between his teeth and tugged at it, leaving behind darkening hickies. I threw my head back as his hands swept along my torso and his fingers found my nipples. He was gentle with them at first but then he pinched them between his thumb and forefinger. As he rolled them from side to side, Jay quickened his pace.

He was sucking me off hard and fast. My cock twitched inside his mouth.

I took his hair and pulled on it, forcing him to suck me even deeper. I could feel myself ramming into the back of his throat. His gagging echoed through the room.

Suddenly, Harvey stopped kissing my neck. I watched as he took off his clothes. He worked at an agonizing pace, making a clear show out of it. I licked my lips, leaned forward, and took his hardened nipple into my mouth.

As my tongue ran along his areola, he groaned in pleasure.

He pushed me away and finished undressing. Once he was naked, he pulled Jay off my cock and yanked him over to the side of the bed where he bent him over, ass in the air.

Harvey had this alpha essence that nearly made me drool. Everything about him was so masculine and sexy.

Naturally, my hand fell to my cock. I wrapped my fingers around my girth and started to stroke myself up and down.

"Mmm, you've got one hell of an ass," Harvey whispered as he leaned down to kiss Jay's cheek. He decorated it with kisses as Jay swayed his hips from side to side. It was quite the sight.

Abruptly, he lifted his hand and smacked that exposed ass cheek. The sound reverberated off the walls. Jay's skin took on a nasty red hue in the shape of Harvey's handprint.

I blinked.

Another crack echoed through the room as Harvey slapped his other ass cheek.

This time, Jay cried out. "Harder!" He begged, back arched.

Harvey grabbed his hair and pulled on it until Jay was forced to look at the ceiling. I shimmied close enough where I could reach out and toy with his nipples. He whimpered as I twisted them to a painful degree. But, between his legs, his cock raged on. He was enjoying himself and so were we.

"Hand me the lube," Harvey demanded.

I quickly complied.

Harvey lathered his fingers with lube. Slowly, he probed the young man's hole until he was eventually able to push his middle finger down to the knuckle. He kept his other hand on the small of Jay's back, pinning him firmly against the bed. Jay could not get away. He was now Harvey's little plaything.

That finger started to move. The pace was gradual. With each second, he picked up the pace.

He twisted his wrist and I imagined he was hooking his finger as well to properly reach Jay's prostate.

"Oh. My. God." Jay moaned through gritted teeth. He clutched at the bed sheets as Harvey added another finger to the mix.

Meanwhile, I ran my thumb along my tip until a droplet of precum oozed from my hole. I guided Jay's head toward the salty treat. His tongue darted out of his mouth and lapped up the drop like he was some sort of addict. "Keep going," I said, my fingers tangled against his hair. "And don't stop until I tell you to stop."

Smack!

Jay jumped, ass cheeks jiggling from the blow. Before he could truly recover, Harvey added a third finger to his tight hole. They moved in perfect unison, finger fucking the young player until he was screaming for mercy.

But Harvey only responded by pulling out his fingers and ramming his cock into his hole.

Jay tensed, toes curling, a silent scream emerging from his lips. I took his face in my hands and kissed him as Harvey slowly made love to him.

Time seemed to stop as I savored every moment. I never thought something like this could happen in real life and yet, here I was in bed with two of the sexiest men on the planet.

And with that thought, I stroked myself harder and harder, ready to shoot my load right into Jay's face.

Chapter 15 Harvey

I could tell by the look on his face that Kalvin was getting close but I couldn't let that happen.

Quickly, I pulled out of Jay and pounced on the fitness trainer. I pinned his wrists above his head. "How about I take you for a little ride?" I whispered into his ear before nibbling on the lobe. "But only if you keep our friend here entertained." As Jay laid down by his side, I guided his hand to Jay's throbbing cock. "Don't stop," I growled. "Or, you're going to regret it."

I took a good helping of lube and slathered it all over his cock until he was nice and slippery. To tease him a bit, I tightened my grip but slowed my pace. His tip was purple with excitement. With my other hand, I fondled his balls. I loved the way he moaned, eyes rolling into the back of his head.

"You're so sexy." I murmured. "Both of you." I stroked him one more time before guiding him toward my entrance. Slowly, I eased myself onto his length inch by inch. Once he was balls deep inside of me, I started to bounce up and down. I was a little awkward to start but I soon got the hang of it.

I had my hands on his chest, using it as a stabilization point as I picked up the pace, going faster and faster. With each thrust, his cock kept hitting against my sweet spot. It took everything I had to keep from screaming.

Meanwhile, Jay writhed with pleasure. He bucked his hips into the air, teeth gritted together.

I slapped his balls ever so lightly and he screamed. The sound only worked to turn me on even more.

Kalvin's cock twitched. "Don't cum," I warned.

I rode him harder and harder until all I could hear was the sound of our balls slapping together. I was breathing hard and it felt like my heart would burst right out of my chest but yet, I didn't even think of stopping.

"Fuck!" Kalvin clawed at the bed. "I'm going to cum."

Abruptly, I pulled away. Kalvin's cock slapped against his stomach. "What did I tell you?" I growled, biting at his left nipple and tugging on it – hard. I flipped him around and smacked his ass.

Jay groaned as he watched us. He kept licking his lips with hunger so I relented my position to him. He jumped behind the personal trainer, took him by the hips, and went to town. He was like an animal who had lost all control. I could see it in his eyes. He growled and snarled, nails running along the man's skin, leaving behind angry red lines.

Now it was my turn to beat it. My cock had never been so hard in my entire life. I thought it would explode at any moment. The sight of these two men going at it drove me absolutely insane.

I couldn't deny my sexuality any longer.

Jay pulled at Kalvin's hair. This seemed to turn him on even more. His body started to shake and I could tell he was just on the brink of climax. So, I reached between his legs and took his balls in my hands. I fondled them between my fingers, adding to his pleasure.

It was too much for the personal trainer. He screamed, back arched, toes curled. His load came out as an eruption that painted the sheets with streaks of white.

Gasping, he struggled to stay on his hands and knees as Jay kept fucking him senseless.

I kissed Kalvin but only for a moment. My balls ached for release and I knew I wouldn't last much longer.

Luckily, a long, drawn-out groan emerged from Jay's lips as he fell forward in his exhaustion. By the time he pulled out of Kalvin's ass, his tip still oozed with precum.

Grinning, I licked it clean before hovering over the two men and stroking myself to climax. I decorated them both with my cum. Oh, what a sight.

My grin deepened as I walked over to the bathroom and handed them a wet washcloth to share among themselves. They were both breathing hard with this glazed-over look on their faces. "How about we enjoy a nice, hot bath together?" I offered.

Before they could answer me, I was already headed that way. I turned on the tap and ensured that it was set for the perfect temperature. As I waited for the tub to fill, Jay walked through the door with this sheepish expression. "That was just... amazing." He settled himself in my lap, arms wrapped around my neck. "I'm sorry."

I shook my head. "No, I should be the one apologizing. I can only imagine what you must have gone through when you saw me with Jamie. I can't even imagine you with someone else. Just the thought of it sends my blood boiling." I said. I gently ran my fingers through his hair. "In fact, I should be thanking you."

"Thanking me?" He cocked his head to the side.

"Well, if it wasn't for you, I never would have come to terms with my sexuality," I admitted. "It's scary to think of how the world will react, but I know as long as you two are by my side, I can get through anything."

He cupped my cheek against his hand and brought me in for a kiss. His lips were as delicious as ever but even more so this time around because I knew I would keep this man forever.

When we pulled away, I looked into his eyes. "So, you aren't going to leave the team, right?"

"I no longer have any reason to do so." He smiled. "I wanted to leave because I couldn't live with the fact that you had rejected me but now..." His smile widened. "I know things will be different and with this kind of chemistry between us, we are bound to kill it on the ice."

"And I'll be cheering from the sidelines." Kalvin chimed in from the doorway. "Don't forget that."

Chapter 16 Jay

A few months later, at the championship game.

Sweat coated my palms forcing me to wipe them clean against the fabric of my pants. I had never felt this nervous before. My stomach was so tied up in knots that it was hard to breathe. I feared I would throw up my lunch at any moment.

"How are you holding up?" Harvey appeared behind me, dressed in his uniform. Somehow, he became sexier and sexier every time I saw him. And, every time he donned that uniform, it filled me with butterflies.

"Okay... I guess, but I am a little nervous." I got up and started to pace in order to use up some of my energy. My fingers had started to shake as the minutes rolled by. I just wanted time to slow down so I could prepare myself for this moment in my mind. "I keep thinking this is just a dream."

"Well, it's not, kid." Chad clapped me on the back. "This is everything we've been waiting for. I hope you're ready. All eyes are gonna be on you, rookie."

"Gee, that makes me feel so much better."

Just then, the coach walked in. He had this serious expression on his face as he looked us all over. "I hope you are all prepared for what's to come. This is the championship game. We win this one and we take home the Stanley Cup." His eyes fell on mine. "Now, this is going to be the first time for some of you. Don't let the pressure get to you. Just think of it like any other game – only a thousand times more important."

I shifted from foot to foot, staggering underneath the intensity of his gaze.

Harvey took my hand and squeezed it. That alone was enough to calm me down. I took a deep breath and focused on clearing my mind of any doubts. I can do this. I can do this. I kept telling myself over and over again. Slowly, my confidence started to build.

I squeezed Harvey's hand and offered a smile in the coach's direction.

He nodded his head. "I'll be counting on you guys so don't let me down." With that, we charged out of the locker room and onto the ice. A bunch of cheerleaders shook their pompoms in introduction.

The air was thick with excitement. Every seat was filled. Hard-core hockey fans had their faces painted with team colors. Children could barely sit still in their parents' laps. Couples wore matching jerseys. To my surprise, there were a few people wearing my number – lucky number 13.

My heart was so loud that it threatened to deafen the thrum of the crowd.

I adjusted my grip on the hockey stick as the rival team joined us on the ice. They seemed much bigger than I remembered. Their faces, even half-hidden behind their helmets, were dark and menacing. Most of them looked like they could squish me with their pinkies.

Sitting in the front row, Kalvin offered a thumbs up. I know it was supposed to encourage me through the game but right now, I just felt sick to my stomach.

The sports announcer was saying something but it was impossible to focus on his words. To me, it sounded like he was speaking a foreign language.

And then, I heard the buzzer.

The puck was dropped and the game began.

Our opponents were good – too good – but we were better.

Our passes were flawless, flying from person to person. The other players never had a chance to steal.

I concentrated on the game and the game alone. Adrenaline pumped through my system. Somehow, my vision became clearer. The air around me seemed crisper.

The puck came my way and I stopped it in its tracks. Skillfully, I spun around, avoiding an incoming tackle from one of the biggest players.

Another one came barreling in my direction but I avoided him too. I had my eyes set on the goal and that was the only thing I could think of.

But in my greed, I lost track of my surroundings and someone grabbed the puck from right under my nose. Before I could properly realize what had happened, he had already scored against our team.

I cursed under my breath.

"Keep your head in the game. We have to work as a team." Harvey shouted my way. "Or we are never going to win this."

I nodded. He was right. I couldn't put the 'I' in team. I had to depend on my fellow hockey players if we had any chance of winning the cup.

So, that's exactly what I did. I put my faith in my team, passing the puck whenever possible. I stuck to my position and made sure that no one got through our defenses and if by some luck, they did, I knew that Harvey was there to help me out.

***

By halftime, the score was tied. It was one hell of a game. Our opponents weren't going down without a fight but then again, neither were we.

But I could tell that they were losing stamina. Their formation wasn't as tight as it was during the first half of the game. It was easier for us to slip through the cracks and by the end, we had quite the lead.

It was all over.

With only a few minutes left on the clock, there was nothing they could do.

The buzzer went off and my heart skipped a beat. I couldn't believe it. We had actually won the championship.

I was swept up in the team huddle. It felt amazing to be a part of the winning circle. I had never felt so high in my entire life.

"We did it!" I screamed alongside everyone else. "We actually did it."

Chapter 17 Harvey

Once the cheering had died down a bit, I took Jay by the hand. I waited until some of the other players had gotten off the ice and we were the only two left.

"What are you doing?" He whispered in my direction.

I just squeezed his hand. I was incredibly nervous. I could sense that all eyes were on me.

One of the cheerleaders returned with a microphone in her hand. "Good luck." She said before scurrying away.

I held it so tightly that my knuckles were bright white. Still, I couldn't back away from this now. I took a deep breath and turned to look at Kalvin who nodded his head.

"Thank you, everyone, for coming out to the game and supporting us." I dropped Jay's hand and did a little circle around the rink so that it felt like I was talking to everyone inside the arena. "It means a lot to the players to have such loving fans."

Jay stood awkwardly in the middle of the ice. He watched me with a look of utter confusion on his face.

"Now I ask for your love and support as I tell you the truth." I returned to Jay and took his hand in mine once more. I laced our fingers together. "Some of you may know me as the league's playboy. I've been on the cover of a few magazines where I'm posed with sexily clad women." There was a pause and a silence washed over the entire building. "But that's all a lie."

The silence intensified.

"I have learned that I'm not a womanizer. I only pretended to be because I was scared of who I really was." I looked out at the crowd. This was the moment of truth. They would either love me or hate me. "And who I am is a man that loves other men." With that, I took Jay into my arms and kissed him for the world to see.

At first, nothing happened, but then, an eruption of applause burst through the arena. Everyone was on their feet, cheering for us.

I smiled against the kiss. No one cared that I was gay. I guess I was scared for no good reason.

***

That night.

"That was one hell of a game, you two," Kalvin commented as we sat down to enjoy our celebratory meal. "If you ask me, it was all due to all that training I put you through." He said with a wink. "If it wasn't for me, you'd still be in the minor leagues."

Jay laughed and reached across the table to squeeze his hand. "I'm sure that's the reason and not Harvey's excellent defending skills." He looked my way with a certain dreaminess in his eyes like he was admiring his childhood hero. "He was like a god on that ice. I've never seen anything like it."

"Keep it up and you're going to make me blush," I said.

"Maybe that was my intention." Jay giggled.

"I think it would be justifiable payback for what you did to him," Kalvin added. "I can't believe you kissed him on the ice like that. It was pretty romantic. I have to admit, I was a little jealous."

I frowned. "Kalvin... I..."

He shook his head. "I'm just pulling your chain. Society can accept gayness but I don't think it's quite ready to accept a three-way relationship. I'm perfectly okay with being the one on the sidelines."

This time it was Jay who shook his head. "You shouldn't feel that way. You're my partner just as much as Harvey is. I love you both equally."

My eyes widened. "Did you just say what I think you said?"

Kalvin nodded. "I think he did."

Jay's cheeks turned a rosy shade of pink. He busied himself by looking at the menu. To his benefit, the waitress came over and told us about the night's specials.

"Can I get you guys anything to drink?"

"Bring over a bottle of your best red wine," I said. "Tonight's a night for celebration."

"Oh?" She asked, cocking her head to the side. "May I ask what you three are celebrating?"

I flashed a charming smile. "I'm guessing that you're not much of a fan of hockey, are you?"

"No, sir, I'm not." She bowed her head in apology. "But my boyfriend is a big fan of the Minute Men. Whenever there's a game, he's always glued to his TV screen."

I chuckled. "Well, believe it or not, I'm the second defenseman for the team, Harvey Price."

"Oh my God! I've heard him talk about you before." She leaned forward until she was standing on the tips of her toes. "Do you think I could get an autograph. It's almost our anniversary and I know he would go nuts."

"Of course." I stole the pen from her pocket and signed my napkin before handing it over to her. "I hope he likes it."

With that, she walked away to get us our bottle of wine.

"You're such a show-off," Jay said with a grin.

"Better get used to it," Kalvin added. "He has an ego the size of the Seattle Space Needle."

"Are you sure you're not confusing that with his junk?" Jay flashed a naughty look in my direction.

"Hmm, maybe." Kalvin laughed. "Anyway, did we come here to chit-chat or did we come here to eat?" He opened up his menu with a dramatic pop.

I smiled to myself. I never thought my life would end this way but I'm glad it did.

Epilogue Jay

Two years later.

We had upgraded to a mini-mansion. It had more than enough room for the three of us but at any given time, we were usually in the same room together, enjoying each other's company.

Today we were by the poolside just soaking up the sun.

"What are you reading?" Kalvin asked as he handed me a long island iced tea.

I tossed a bookmark between the pages and placed it on a nearby table. "Oh, nothing really. I was trying to dive into the classics but I don't think I'm much of a fan."

"War and Peace, huh?" Kalvin mused. "It's a pretty big book."

Harvey emerged from the water and stole my drink. Before I could stop him, half of it was gone. "Ah."

"Hey, that was mine!" I protested but he silenced my qualms with a kiss. It took me by surprise. My breath was stolen away as I melted against his body. All else faded away as my lips danced against his.

Kalvin disappeared into the house, probably to make me another drink.

Harvey slithered his hands underneath my ass and held it tight between his fingers. I moaned into the kiss, heart racing with desire. No matter how much time we spent together, I still wanted more. I was addicted to these men like they were narcotics.

Suddenly, he hoisted me in his arms. Our kiss intensified. My mind turned to mush as my lungs burned. Even so, I didn't think of pulling away.

And then, he threw me into the pool. I sunk to the bottom like I was made out of lead. When I opened my eyes, there was Harvey. He swam over to me and kissed me. While our lips were locked, we floated up to the surface.

"You know, my phone was in my pocket." I griped.

"We can just buy you a new one. We have the money. Both of us are sponsored now and even Kalvin has that contract with the smoothie blender. Things are pretty good for us right now. I don't think a water-logged phone is going to break the bank." We headed over to the shallow end of the pool where Harvey held me by the hips.

I had my legs wrapped around his hips. It felt so natural to be with this man like he was the soul mate I had been looking for all my life.

"Speaking of phones, do you know what I saw on my newsfeed this morning?" He asked.

"No, what did you see?" I traced my fingers along his collarbone. He shifted in delight. After two years together, I knew exactly what he liked and he didn't. I could make him moan and scream in under a minute flat and he could do the same to me.

"Do you remember Jamie?"

Just her name was enough to sour my mood. Memories of her on Harvey's lap plagued my mind.

Harvey pulled me a little closer. "You have nothing to worry about. She means nothing to me, you know that."

I nodded. He was right. There was no reason for me to be jealous. Harvey had been nothing but faithful during our years together. It was unfair of me to doubt him.

"Well, I saw that she just recently got married."

"Let me guess, she snagged some hockey player." I guessed. "Probably Chad."

He shook his head. "Even Chad wouldn't stoop that low. Besides, I think he has a girlfriend – maybe even a kid. You're a little behind on the times."

"Sorry." I rubbed the back of my neck. "I don't really pay attention to locker room conversations anymore. Most of the time, they are pretty pointless."

"So, anyway, she got married – to Coach Morrison."

"You're kidding me. When did that happen?"

"Yesterday. They eloped to some Caribbean island." He said. "She did it for the money. I don't know why anyone else would marry that loaf."

"Hey, maybe she genuinely liked him," I suggested although I knew it was far from the truth.

He scoffed. "She's a gold digger – no doubt about it. When I asked her on a date, she wanted me to bring my fancy car and she insisted on a fancy Italian restaurant. Some people – that's all they want."

"What are you two talking about?" Kalvin returned with a fresh iced tea and a tray of pretzels. "I figured you guys might be a little peckish."

"Hey, at least it's not celery this time," I said.

Kalvin shook his head. "When are you two going to stop complaining about my food? I'm just trying to keep you both healthy. If you insist on eating chicken wings and pizza then we have to work five times as hard in the gym."

"I think it's worth it," Harvey said, backing me up.

"You two are impossible." Kalvin sat down on the edge of the pool. "And yet, I manage to love you."

I smiled. "I love you too, Kalvin."

"So, what were you guys talking about just then." He repeated.

"Well..." I grabbed my drink and took a sip. "Maybe Harvey should tell you."

"Coach Morrison married an old admirer of mine."

"Let me guess – Jamie." He said casually.

"How did you know?" I asked, raising an eyebrow in question.

"She goes to my gym so I overheard her talking about it with some of her girlfriends. She was bragging about the fact that he was loaded and how she would never have to work a day in her life."

"See, what did I tell you. She's a gold digger." Harvey chirped triumphantly. "I am so glad that I dodged that bullet."

I smiled. "So am I."

Suddenly, he yanked Kalvin in the water. "There, that's better."

Once Kalvin regained his composure, Harvey reeled us in for a big bear hug. His grip was so tight that I could barely breathe. Still, it was nice to feel his warmth against my body. I leaned my head on Kalvin's shoulder and even through the chlorine I could smell his vegan deodorant. It was a strong scent but it was growing on me.

"Thank you." Harvey kissed the top of my head and then Kalvin's. "You two have done nothing but make my life better. I never thought I would find my way into a three-way gay relationship but hey, I'm not complaining."

Kalvin smiled. "I have to admit, being with you guys is much better than I expected. We have yet to get into a real fight and the sex is as good as ever."

I grinned. "You got that right. Here's to the future, may we stay this happy for an eternity."

*****

Don't miss out!

Visit the website below and you can sign up to receive emails whenever Van Cole publishes a new book. There's no charge and no obligation.

https://books2read.com/r/B-A-RTRV-LPTDC

BOOKS 2 READ

Connecting independent readers to independent writers.

Also by Van Cole

3 Man Huddle: MMM Best Friend Romance
His Alpha Wolf: Gay First Time Romance
A Dragon's Miracle: Gay Dragon MPREG Romance
Double-Teamed: MMM First Time Football Romance
His Football Star: Gay Second Chance Romance
Love In My Town: MM First Time Romance
Training A Hockey Star
Game Night
Double Shift
Take A Shot
Dear Professor
Getting Inked
Ninth Inning
Triple Threat
Seducing My Best Friend's Brother
My Protector
The Blueprint
Show Me The Way
End Zone
Matched To His Tiger
Love At First Puck
My Straight Boss
Falling For The Alpha
My Boss
On Thin Ice

www.ingramcontent.com/pod-product-compliance
Lightning Source LLC
Chambersburg PA
CBHW051254160726
47994CB00003B/1163